Every night the sky twinkled with stars.
And every night the sheep slept
under them.

But one night
something
very strange
happened . . .

A mysterious star began to fall from the sky.

It got closer
and closer
until . . .

BOO

M!

As the smoke cleared, the sheep saw
what looked like a jetpack and . . .

a little cow!

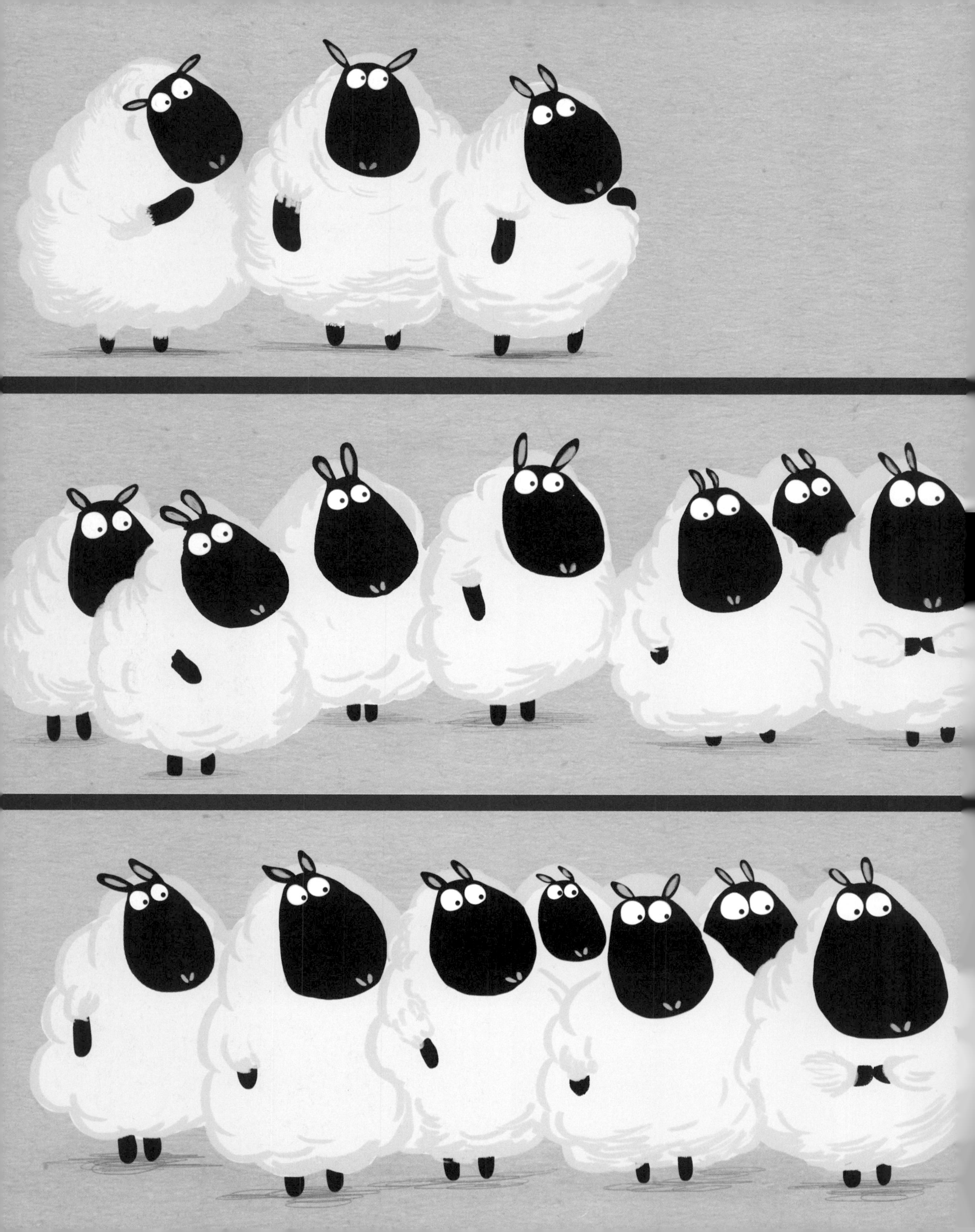

At first, the
little cow was
very confused.

But the sheep gave
it a blanket and
a hot cup of tea,
which helped.

"Where are you from,
little cow?" they asked.
"What's your name?"

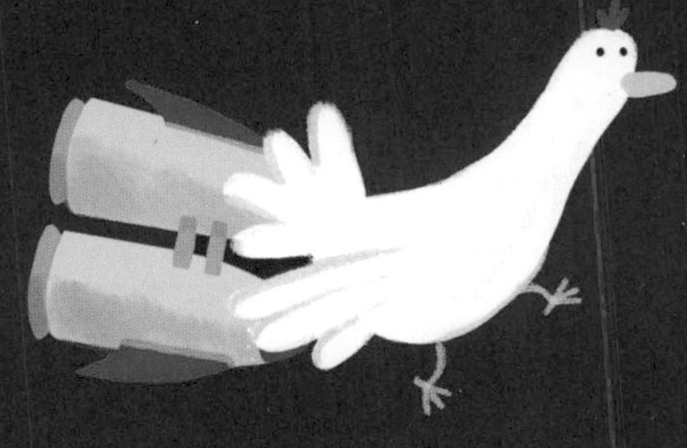

The little cow told the sheep everything.
It was quite a story.

But the sheep couldn't understand a word the cow was saying. It just seemed to be making weird noises.

"Let's call it Dave," agreed the sheep. "HELLO, DAVE!"

Dave could see she had a problem.

Surely Bertha the cow would understand?
"Mooo?" tried Bertha.
"Wooo!" replied Dave.
"Nope," said Bertha. "I don't know what it's on about."

“It can’t be from around here,” said Kevin the cat.

“No idea!” said Rufus the dog.

Meanwhile Pamela the pig had just woken up and didn’t know *what* was going on.

If nobody could understand her,
how on earth would Dave get back home?

Hang on . . .

What was that?

A countdown?

Dave had a funny
feeling about this . . .

The chickens had been busy. And now they were going to boldly go where no chicken had gone before.

Dave watched her jetpack zoom up into the sky. Then something slowly floated down to the ground.

It was a photo of Dave
with her family at home –
on the MOON!

"Oh, you're a MOON COW,"
said the sheep. "Well, why
didn't you say so? Let's get
you home."

Without Dave's jetpack, getting to the moon was going to be tricky.

They tried jumping,

climbing

and balancing.

But nothing worked.

Dave just didn't know what to do.

She stood under the moon and called out.

One by one, the sheep joined her.

Something twinkled.

And soon a star began to fall from the sky!

It got closer and closer until . . .

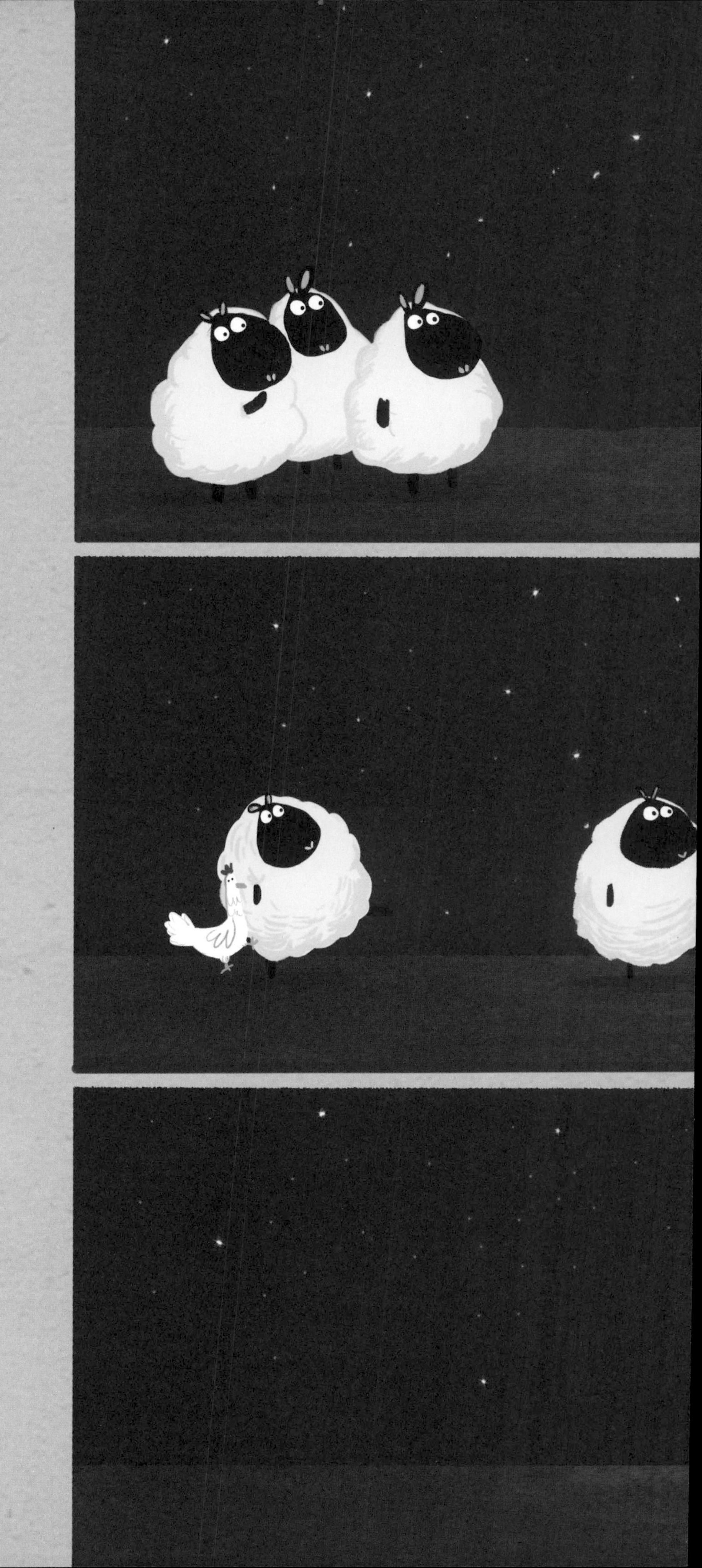

WOOO!

The moon cows had heard them!

Dave told the moon cows
all about her adventure,
and they understood
every word she said.

Soon it was time for Dave
to go back home.

Everyone cheered as she
zoomed up into the
night sky.

Now, every night before they go to sleep, the sheep look up at the moon and say goodnight to Dave . . .

And sometimes,
when the night is
quiet and still . . .

. . . they think they can
hear her calling back.